**I'd like to dedicate this book
to octopuses everywhere.
Peace & Love,
Ringo**

**For Ruth, Johnny, and Anna
with all my love.
Ben Cort**

ALADDIN

An imprint of Simon & Schuster Children's Publishing Division

1230 Avenue of the Americas, New York, NY 10020

First Aladdin hardcover edition February 2014

Text copyright © 2013 by Universal Music Publishing International/Startling Music Ltd.

Illustrations copyright © 2013 by Ben Cort

Jacket designed by Karin Paprocki

Originally published in Great Britain in 2013 by Simon & Schuster UK Ltd.

For information about special discounts for bulk purchases, please contact Simon & Schuster Special Sales at

1-866-506-1949 or business@simonandschuster.com.

The Simon & Schuster Speakers Bureau can bring authors to your live event.

For more information or to book an event contact the Simon & Schuster Speakers Bureau at

1-866-248-3049 or visit our website at www.simonspeakers.com.

Manufactured in China 1013 LEO

2 4 6 8 10 9 7 5 3 1

Full CIP data for this book is available from the Library of Congress.

ISBN 978-1-4814-0362-7 • ISBN 978-1-4814-0363-4 (eBook)

OCTOPUS'S Garden

Ringo Starr

Illustrated by Ben Cort

ALADDIN
NEW YORK LONDON TORONTO SYDNEY NEW DELHI

I'd like to be under the sea
    In an octopus's garden in the shade.

He'd let us in, knows where we've been
In his octopus's garden in the shade.

I'd ask my friends to come and see
An octopus's garden with me.

I'd like to be under the sea
   In an octopus's garden in the shade.

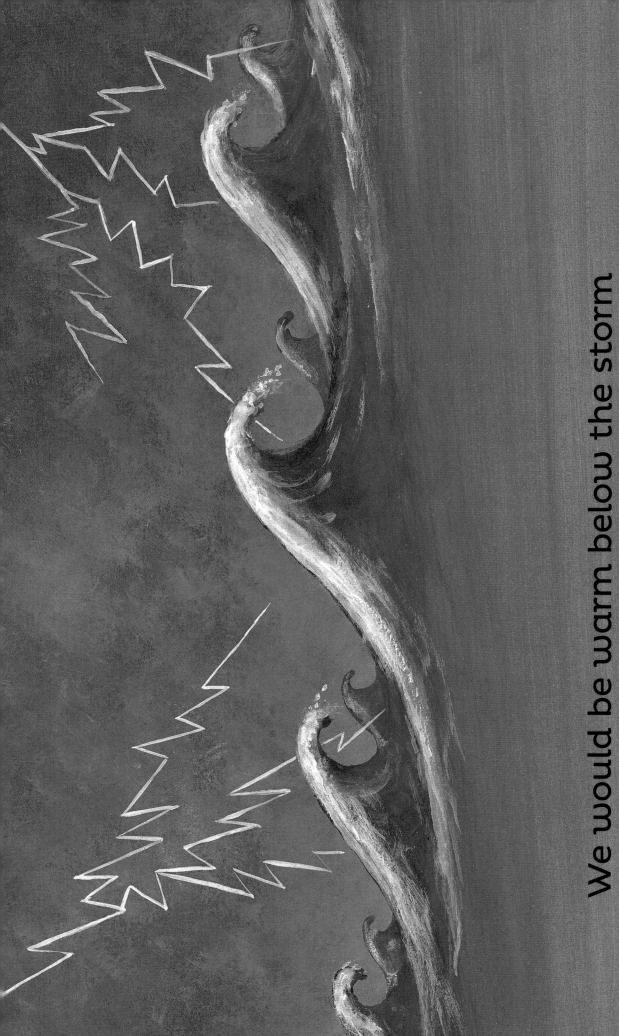

We would be warm below the storm

In our little hideaway beneath the waves.

Resting our head on the seabed
In an octopus's garden near a cave.

We would sing and dance around
Because we know we can't be found.

I'd like to be under the sea
In an octopus's garden in the shade.

We would shout and swim about
The coral that lies beneath the waves
(Lies beneath the ocean waves).

Oh what joy for every girl and boy
Knowing they're happy and they're safe
(Happy and they're safe).

We would be so happy you and me
No one there to tell us what to do.

I'd like to be under the sea
   In an octopus's garden with YOU.